I See Spring

by Charles Ghigna

illustrated by Ag Jatkowska

PICTURE WINDOW BOOKS
a capstone imprint

I see raindrops falling down.

I see raincoats blue and brown.

I see dark clouds way up high.

I see a rainbow in the sky.

I see puddles in the street.

I see rain boots on my feet.

I see sunshine on the trees.

I see bluebirds ride the breeze.

I see robins build a nest.

I see bunnies take a rest.

I see ladybugs and snails.

I see puppies chase their tails.

I see yellow daffodils.

I see bluebells on the hills.

I see squirrels scamper on the ground.

I see pinwheels go round and round.

I see kites up in the sky.

I see clothes hanging up to dry.

I see butterflies and flowers.

I see signs of more spring showers!

The End

—for Charlotte and Christopher

I See is published by Picture Window Books
A Capstone Imprint
1710 Roe Crest Drive
North Mankato, Minnesota 56003
www.capstonepub.com

Library of Congress Cataloging-in-Publication Data
Ghigna, Charles.
  I see spring / by Charles Ghigna ; illustrated by AG Jatkowska.
      p. cm.
  Summary: Illustrations and easy-to-read, rhyming text show what makes
spring special, from raindrops and robins to bluebells and butterflies.
ISBN 978-1-4048-6587-7 (library binding)
ISBN 978-1-4048-6849-6 (pbk.)
 [1. Stories in rhyme. 2. Spring—Fiction.] I. Jatkowska, Ag, ill. II. Title.
  PZ8.3.G345Iap 2011
  [E]—dc22
                                        2010050094

Creative Director: Heather Kindseth

Designer: Emily Harris

Printed in the United States of America in North Mankato, Minnesota.
022012
006603R